Is My Friend at Home?

IS MY FRIEND AT HOME?

PUEBLO FIRESIDE TALES

RETOLD BY John Bierhorst ∘ PICTURES BY Wendy Watson

Farrar Straus Giroux NEW YORK

ACKNOWLEDGMENTS

The fireside tales in this book are trickster
stories originally told in the Hopi pueblos of Arizona.
Winter was the time for storytelling, especially after dark when
the Sun was traveling under the earth. Although the tricksters are animals,
it is said that if they take off their skins they become immediately human.
Source: H. R. Voth, *The Traditions of the Hopi*, Field Museum, Anthropological
Series, vol. 8; with help from E. S. Curtis, *The North American Indian*,
vol. 12; F. H. Cushing, *Zuñi Breadstuff*; and W. D. Wallis, "Folk Tales
from Shumopovi," *Journal of American Folklore*, vol. 49.

Text copyright © 2001 by John Bierhorst
Illustrations copyright © 2001 by Wendy Watson
Distributed in Canada by Douglas & McIntyre Ltd.
Color separations by Photolitho AG, Gossau-Zürich
Printed and bound in the United States of America by Berryville Graphics
Design and typography by Jane Byers Bierhorst
First edition, 2001
1 3 5 7 9 10 8 6 4 2

Library of Congress Cataloging-in-Publication Data
Bierhorst, John.
    Is my friend at home? : Pueblo fireside tales
retold by John Bierhorst ; pictures by Wendy Watson.
        p. cm.
    Summary: A collection of traditional tales originally told in the
Hopi pueblos of Arizona, featuring animal characters.
    ISBN 0-374-33550-8
    1. Hopi Indians Folklore. 2. Tales–Arizona.
[1. Hopi Indians Folklore. 2. Indians of North America–Arizona
Folklore. 3. Folklore–Arizona.] I. Watson, Wendy, ill. II. Title.
E99.H7B464   2001
398.2'089'9745–dc21
    [E]   99-29214

In the evening the Sun touches
the ocean in the west and climbs
down the long ladder to the underworld.
Then he sets out on his underground journey
to the sunrise place in the east. Up above,
now that the world is dark, the time
has come for people to light
fires and tell stories.

∘ Roasted Ears ∘

Shall I begin?
Yes.

A tale of the grandfathers, long ago. Badger and Coyote were friends.

When Coyote visited Badger, meat would be served. Both Coyote and Badger were great hunters.

One day, when Coyote had eaten well at his friend Badger's, he asked, "What is this delicious food?"

"I wanted to give you something special," said his friend, "so I cut off my ears and roasted them for you. By the time you got here, my ears had grown back again, and now I feel fine."

At first Coyote wouldn't believe. "You didn't," he said. "And yet you say you did."

"I did," said his friend. "Look, I am not completely well yet," and he showed him a faint scratch on his head that he had made earlier with his knife.

Coyote believed. "Come visit me tomorrow," he said, "and I will have something special for you, too." He thought he would outdo his friend Badger, because in those days Coyote had ears as long as a rabbit's. When he had gone, his friend said to himself, "Coyote believes easily."

The next morning Coyote got up early and sharpened his knife. He built a fire, cleaned his roasting pot, and put it down in its sitting place. "Now!" he said. "No, wait. I had better close my eyes. I can't stand to look." He closed his eyes. "Now!" he said, and he sliced off both ears with a single stroke. Just at that moment a gust of wind came up, and the ears-that-were blew away.

When Badger arrived, the pot was still empty and they had nothing to eat.

And that's the story. Well, no. There's one more part. It goes: Ever since that day, Coyote's ears have been short.

◦ Why Mouse Walks Softly ◦

Listen!
YES?

Mouse had two friends, Coyote and Beetle. They came often, to renew the breath of friendship. "But what will I feed them when they come tomorrow?" Mouse was asking herself. She was not a great hunter, and her storerooms were empty.

Mouse thought deeply. Then her thoughts turned to the village. As soon as it was dark, she ran to the big houses. Finding dried fat, she broke off a piece and carried it home.

In another house she found antelope meat and made many noisy trips, racing back and forth.

In still another house she found wafer bread. "Thanks, here's wafer bread!" she cried. "And grease cakes!" She hurried home with first one piece and then another, racing both ways.

When at last she lay down to rest, white dawn had appeared. Just as the Sun was standing up, Coyote and Beetle arrived.

"Have you come?" said Mouse. "I have plenty to eat."

"Yes, we have come."

"We had better start eating early," said Mouse, bragging. "I have plenty!" But while she was serving the food, she suddenly fell into dreams, worn out from her many trips.

"What is your heart up to?" said Coyote to Beetle.

"It's angry," said Beetle. "Mouse brags too much. Shall we tangle her up with a song?"

"Yes," said Coyote.

Just then Mouse woke up again. "We have a song for you,"
said Beetle.

> night is coming
>
> Mouse starts running
>
> close your windows, big people
>
> dawn is coming
>
> Mouse keeps running
>
> close your windows, big people

At first Mouse was angry. Then she said to herself, "The whole
village knows where I've been. I've made too much noise." From then
on Mouse walked softly.

And she is still doing it.

° Beetle's New Life °

Listen.
WE'RE LISTENING!

°

Beetle had been living at Grass Ditch since early summer. But now the fire in his house was very low, and he was feeling too cold and too lazy to go out for firewood. In the afternoons, when he used to be singing happily, he would now be pitying himself, singing, "Oh oh, oh oh."

One day, toward noon, Mole came. As he reached the door to Beetle's house, he called, "Ha-o! Is my friend at home?"

"Thanks that you have come," said Beetle softly. Mole went in and sat by the fire, but it was too low to make him feel warm. "I am only living a very little now," said Beetle, pitying himself.

"Badger has medicine," said Mole. "I will go find him." Then he ran up the ladder with thoughts of healing.

When he got to Badger's, he shouted, "Ha-o! Are you there?" He was breathing hard. "Beetle is only half alive. Will you come soon?"

"Yes," said Badger. Then he put on his sash and his medicine pouch. "Mole," he said, "you carry this blanket."

When they got to Beetle's house, the fire was so low it was almost not burning. "Now then, I have come to you," said Badger. There was no answer.

"Do you think the breath has gone out?" asked Mole.

"The breath has gone out," said Badger gravely. "But it will not be gone long." Opening his pouch, he took out medicine and put a little on Beetle's lips. He put some in each of his ears and on top of his heart. "Mole," he said, "pass me that blanket." Mole passed the blanket, and Badger spread it over Beetle's body.

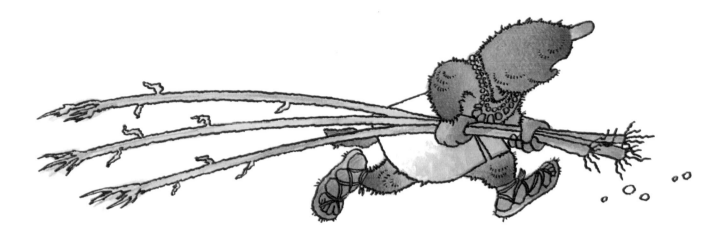

Then Mole said out loud, "I think I should build up this fire." "Run quick!" he said to himself, and he ran outside and found sunflower stalks. He carried them to the fire and built it up. Then the fire's brightness fell over the room.

After a while the blanket began to move. "My medicine is good," said Badger. "The breath has come back." When he took the blanket away, Beetle stood up and was well. "Thanks that you are no longer dead," said Mole. "Dead?" said Beetle. "I think I was just cold."

"May you live strong," said Badger. "You have entered a new trail of life."

"Thanks," said Beetle. Turning to Mole, he said, "Mole, thanks that you have built up my fire."

· Winter Story ·

Let it be about Coyote.
Then listen.

It was long ago. Coyote was a friend of Snake's. They visited each other often.

One day Snake came to Coyote's and said, "I have grown since I was here last. I can't fit into your house anymore."

"I'll go out so you can come in," said Coyote. "We'll talk through the door. I don't want you to be cold."

Snake went inside and circled around the fire. Soon the house was well filled. Outside, Coyote grew colder and colder.

"I hope you are warm enough," said Coyote. But he said it with his lips only. In his heart he was saying, "My friend is dangerous. He wants me to freeze. How can I get even with him?"

The next day, when Snake had gone, Coyote ran to the timber and came back with a load of cedar bark. Warming himself beside the fire, he twisted the bark and made a long addition to his tail. Then he left to go visiting and arrived at Snake's.

"My friend!" said Snake. "Come in!"

"How can I do it?" said Coyote. "You have such a small house."

Snake looked out and saw Coyote's tail stretching into the distance. "Well," he said, "I'll go out so you can come in. I don't want you to be cold. You are my only friend." But in his heart he was thinking what to do.

When it was time to leave, Coyote began to drag his long tail out through the door. Before he had completely left, Snake went partway in and pushed the tip of Coyote's tail against the hot coals.

"Happy journey," called Snake. "May you travel good roads."

"Thanks," called Coyote.

On the way home Coyote's tail burned up. Before the fire was out, it had scorched his fur. "Snake did this," said Coyote to himself. "I'll soften his hard skull."

But when he got back to Snake's house, Snake had shed his skin and filled it with stones. Coyote was fooled. "You animal!" he cried. Then he bit Snake on the head. But he bit into stones, and the stones broke all his teeth.

"Murder!" cried Coyote, and he ran out the door and never came back. And that's why Coyote's teeth look broken. And that's how Snake lost his only friend.

·The Racer·

LOOK, THERE'S A MOUSE!
No. That's the racer.
WHO IS THAT, UNCLE?
Well, she lived long ago. And she brought warm weather.
HOW COULD A MOUSE BRING WARM WEATHER?
Shall I tell it?
YES.

It was long ago. There was deep snow. It was warm where the cicadas
lived, but no one could reach them. Coyote tried but sank down in the

deep drifts. Then he said to Mouse, "You are not heavy. You are swift. Be the racer!"

"I'll try," said Mouse, and she raced over the snow to the cicadas' house. "Come visit us!" she cried.

"Very well," they answered, and they brought their flutes. As they chirped on the flutes, running along behind Mouse, the snow melted, and spring came.

That's why, to this day, people throw cicada wings on the fire in winter. The smoke makes spring come faster.

◦ Why Peaches Are Sweet ◦

Listen.
YES?

It was long ago. At the edge of a peach orchard Dove had a house. Bee was living at Sandy Flat. They knew each other, but not very well. One day, while Dove was picking up peaches in the orchard, she saw Bee and cried out, "Come here. We want to be friends, don't we?"

"Whatever my friend thinks, that's what I think, too," said Bee.

"Come visit me tomorrow," said Dove, "and I will have something good for you to eat."

That night, as she was falling asleep, Bee kept wondering, "What will the food be?" She was hungry. When the Sun came up, she set out immediately, afraid she might be late. In those days bees had no wings and had to walk along the ground.

At last she got to the other side of the orchard and found Dove's house in a crack between two rocks.

"Whose footsteps do I hear?" asked Dove. "Come in!" And she swept a clean place on the floor and laid out food. It was peaches. "Loosen your belt," she said. "Sit and eat. Be satisfied!"

Bee began to eat, but very slowly. Then she shook her head and bit her lips until her chin nearly touched her nose-tip.

"Don't you like what you're eating?" asked her friend.

"I was just thinking," said Bee. "Shall I make some medicine for the peaches?" In those days peaches were not sweet the way they are now. They were always sour.

"Go ahead, make them some medicine," said Dove. "Then maybe I will like them better myself." So Bee put a little honey on the peaches, and for the first time they were sweet.

"Thanks," said Dove. "I will do something for you, too." Then she pulled out a few of her feathers, made wings, and attached them to Bee. "Wear these," she said. "You have earned them. Now fly."

"How can I do it?"

"Just stretch your front legs."

Bee stretched her legs, the wings moved, and she flew away. Since that time, bees have been able to fly. And peaches have been sweet.

Now, that's the story.

∘Coyote Breaks His Leg∘

ONE MORE STORY OF THE GRANDFATHERS?
My word-pouch is empty.
FEEL IN THE BOTTOM OF IT, THEN.
Ha! Did you ever hear how Mouse was a doctor?
NO, NEVER.
Then listen.

It was long ago. Coyote and Badger were hunting. Coyote fell and broke his leg. But Badger ran on, paying no attention; Coyote's cries were like wind in his ears.

Just then Coyote noticed a light. Looking down through an opening in the ground, he saw Mouse sitting next to her fire. The room was large, because Mouse did not live alone. She had many relatives. And there were inner rooms besides.

"How can I come in?" asked Coyote. "My thighbone is broken."

Then Mouse called to her relatives, and they all ran up the ladder and carried Coyote down.

"Could you find me a doctor?" he asked.

"He does not know that we are doctors," whispered the relatives. "Shall we heal him?"

While some were whispering, others were running to one of the inner rooms and bringing out rattles. All those with rattles crowded close to Coyote. The rest swarmed over his body and began to rub. Those who were rubbing sang doctors' songs, and those who were not rubbing just shook their rattles. The whole room echoed with the sound of healing.

When they were finished, Coyote was strong again, ready to go on his way. He was grateful.

"I hope there will be a way to repay you," he said.

"There is always a way," said Mouse. "You are generous. You have much."

"Ah!" said Coyote. "I will leave food next to the fire. You must come soon."

"Thanks," said Mouse. And she did. And she's doing it still.

Now, that's the story.

The Sun has come to the end of his
underground journey. As he climbs up the
ladder to the sunrise place, he puts on the skin of
a gray fox, and white dawn comes up. "Ha!" he cries and
he puts on the skin of a yellow fox, and yellow dawn
comes up. He steps out of the underworld.
It becomes morning. No more
storytelling until nightfall.